The Purchase of Small Secrets

Poems by David Harrison
Illustrated by Meryl Henderson

Wordsong
Boyds Mills Press

To Sandy, with love
—D. L. H.

In memory of my mom and dad,
who taught me to love and respect all living things.
—M. H.

Published by Wordsong
Boyds Mills Press, Inc.
A Highlights Company
815 Church Street
Honesdale, Pennsylvania 18431
Printed in Mexico

Publisher Cataloging-in-Publication Data
Harrison, David L.
The purchase of small secrets / poems by David L. Harrison ;
illustrated by Meryl Henderson.—1st. ed.
[48]p. : ill. ; cm.
Summary: A collection of poems about growing up in the countryside.
ISBN 1-56397-054-6
1. Country life—Juvenile poetry. 2. Children's poetry, American.
[1. Country life—Poetry. 2. American poetry.] I. Henderson, Meryl, ill.
II. Title.
811.54—dc21 1998 AC CIP
Library of Congress Cataloging-in-Publication Data 97-77903

First edition, 1998
Book designed by Tim Gillner
The text of this book is set in 13-point Berkeley.
The illustrations are done in pencil.

10 9 8 7 6 5 4 3 2 1

CONTENTS

Whistling in Spring 5
Talking to the Woods in Spring 6
Initiation 8
A Hole in the Ground 9
Old Man McGrew 10
The Reward 11
Handling Lessons 12
The Crossing 13
Mystery Story 14
Eloise 15
The Price of Honor 16
At the Top of the Ladder 17
Me Down Here 18
Leaving Corky 19
Clucking Away the Day 20
Buckeye Lucky 21
Treed 22
Treasure Hunter 23
Cow Pie Jewels 24
Meeting on a Gravel Bar 25
Looking Down Instead of Up 26
Looking Up Instead of Down 27
Today I Had To 28
Whose Tree Is This? 29
Infield Chatter 30
Plate Talk 32
Market Bound 34
Footprints 35
Qualities of Darkness 36
Journal Entry 38
A Chip of Flint 39
Confidence 40
Beginner's Luck 41
Home-grown 42
A Question of Control 44
The Fisherman 45
Bright-Eyed Good-byes 46
The Purchase of Small Secrets 48

Whistling in Spring

In the top
of my cedar tree
a redbird
is announcing spring,
whistling it in.

Spring is coming!

Whistling in spring
is important business.

Spring is coming!
Spring is coming!

It takes practice
to get it right.

Whistling in spring
is important business!

Spring is coming!
Spring is coming!
Spring is coming!
Spring is coming!

Talking to the Woods in Spring

We weren't worth much
last fall

Me
my sweater torn
wriggling through
barbed wire
a thief caught in the act
coming to steal
your forsaken nests
and drowsing cocoons

You
baldheaded tired
waiting forlornly for
frostbite
to nip your
gnarly trunks and
numb your
crooked fingers

We weren't worth much
last fall
but look at us now!

You
your new leaf curls
done up
in a tight permanent
perfumed and ready
for the spring dance
sap like warm blood rising
tingling your fingertips

Me
sun drunk with
possibilities
dreams leaping like jonquils
my spirits sweetening
as yours
racing expectantly up from my
bare hungry toes

It's going to be
a growing
year!

I feel it
in my
roots!

Don't you?

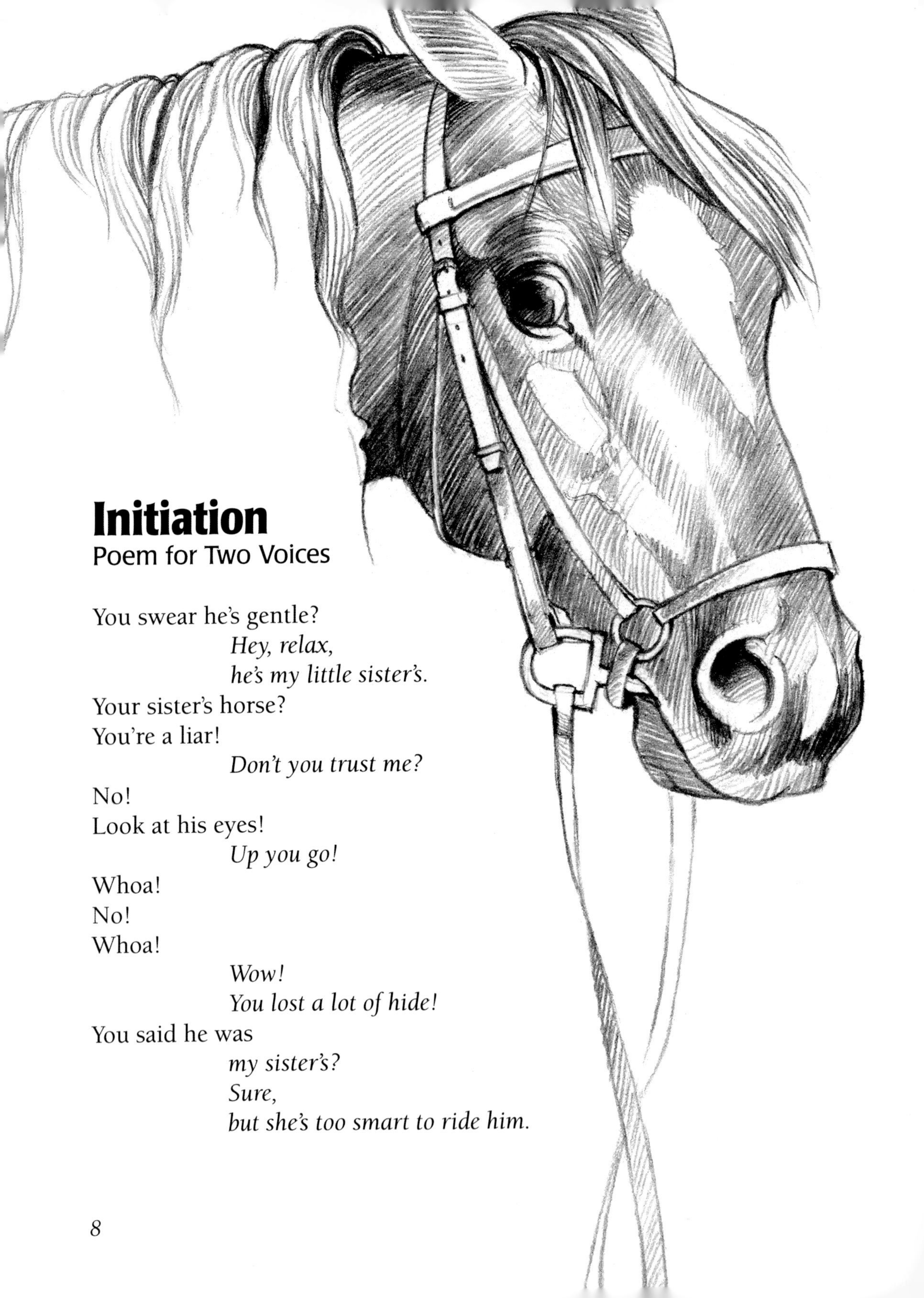

Initiation

Poem for Two Voices

You swear he's gentle?
    Hey, relax,
    he's my little sister's.
Your sister's horse?
You're a liar!
    Don't you trust me?
No!
Look at his eyes!
    Up you go!
Whoa!
No!
Whoa!
    Wow!
    You lost a lot of hide!
You said he was
    my sister's?
    Sure,
    but she's too smart to ride him.

A Hole in the Ground

What creature
tilled the grass
to tunnel here?

A hole in the ground
always makes me wonder.

Is this one empty,
choked with dirt
that trickles through the roof
and rattles down abandoned halls?

Or is something there,
heart pounding,
sniffing me
down in the dark?

A hole in the ground
always makes me wonder.

Old Man McGrew

I've never seen old man McGrew in person.
(People call him that behind his back.)
There's also lots of other stuff they call him
like bony, crooked, grizzled, stubborn, gruff . . .

And poor!
        They say he lives on cans of dog food!
Maybe it's true he's crazy.
                    Who could tell?

Well now he's wandered off or something's happened
and a manhunt's on to find old man McGrew.

Dick said, "Open some dog food, he'll come running."
But it won't be funny if someone finds him dead.

The Reward

Knee-deep in alfalfa
my horse snorts
at going so slow.

Billy to the right
Dick on the left
we fan out like the men
but not so far we'd miss
what we're looking for.

No one's seen old man McGrew
since Sunday.

Billy and Dick lean over their saddles
like hawks after rabbits.
A hundred dollars is a lot of money.

It's hot.
I don't feel good.
Pushing up my glasses, I squint at the sky.
This one time please don't let me win.

Handling Lessons

"It's easy," he says.
"Grab his tail with one hand
and his belly with the other.
A snake won't bite
if you do it right."

Tentatively I take
the tail
from his confident fingers.

Carefully I accept
the whole
sinuous weight.

Muscles coil,
spring,
needles stab my hand!
I yell and throw
at the same time!

"Sorry!" he says,
but he can't stop laughing.

The Crossing

Beside the road
a rabbit crouches to spring.
I step closer, stop,
spot the ruined nose,
blood dried in a string.

Bounced off a car I suppose,
died here watching the road
still posed for flight
when the path seemed clear.

I shake my head,
imagining so many creatures
dead beside some road,
and wonder how to count their loss.
I wish they had no roads to cross.

Mystery Story

The stony, dry riverbed
twists and turns between steep banks
like a dinosaur backbone
curling in the sun.

Feeling Indian,
I find a bone chip,
maybe a skull fragment,
thinner than my breakfast cornflake.

Holding it up, I wonder,
what's your story?
Did you die in combat
miles away,
years ago?
How did you come to haunt this place?

Crouching on stones from the past,
I wonder, what's your story?
What I wouldn't give to know!

Eloise

I did it!
I winked at Eloise!
I winked at Eloise Minor!

I've been sort of . . .
goose bumpish . . .
feverish . . .
thinking how much I love her.

Eloise blushed
and I feel fine!
This calls for another wink
tomorrow.

The Price of Honor

"You cheated!" he shouted.
"I didn't!" I yelled,
shoving him.

He hit me so hard
my nose went snap
and I grabbed him
and we fell on his arm.

"Stop!" he yelled.
"You broke my arm!"
"You take it back?"
"Yeah!" he cried.

Yesterday
we fought for honor.

Today
we're paying the price.

At the Top of the Ladder

At the top of the ladder
half-wild cats
raise suspicious kittens.

Nail hole sunbeams
shine thin floodlights
on hay dust floating like snow.

The base of the ladder
resting below
is a world away.

Up here it's bales and pulleys,
secretive stirrings,
spiders big as berries.

Go softly in a barn loft.
It's a place to whisper.

Me Down Here

Crows
conferring
calling circling

Crossing
the pasture
posting guards

Telling
one another
secrets

Me
uninvited
craving secrets

Me
down here
envying crows

Leaving Corky

I stand with the car door open.
"Corky!" I call out across the fields.
"Here kitty, kitty, kitty, kitty!"

"Time to go."
Dad's voice is quiet.
"Just one more hour," I beg.
"He's been gone a month already," he says.
"Probably chewed up again."

The car eases down the dirt drive.
I stare out the window,
leaving a mind trail,
but in my heart I know.

I'll never see him again,
never know if he's alive,
never be able to explain.

Leaving Corky,
I'm too sad to cry.

Clucking Away the Day

Banana cream pie clouds
baking in the sun,
last tasty morsels
melting in the blue.

Chewing grass, I watch,
content as a hen on her nest,
clucking away the day.

Buckeye Lucky

Talk about lucky!
Buckeye lucky!
That's old lucky me!

I found this perfect
brown black buckeye,
smooth hard
never fails
bring-you-luck buckeye!

Think I'd ever sell her?
Not for a dollar!

Talk about lucky!
Buckeye lucky!
Lucky old buckeye!
Lucky old me!

Treed

There's a squirrel
up that tree

Darned if I
can spot him

Could have shot him
on the ground

Chattering
scattering leaves

But up that tree
he disappeared quick

Good trick!

Maybe he thinks
being up a tree

Is a good place
to be

Treasure Hunter

Walking down
from the ridge
I reach a round glade
sloping off toward the woods
and wonder
how many tales
have been told
in this secret kingdom,
how many mice
have slipped inside
the insincere smiles of snakes.

On this round stage
countless cautious things
have left their tracks
or bones.

I search for scraps
missed
by the cleanup crews
of beetles and worms.

My toe finds it first.
I can't believe my luck!

How long has it been here
perfect, empty, lifeless
whitewashed with age?

Reverently
I pick it up
and turn back
toward the ridge
cradling my newest treasure,
my turtle shell.

Cow Pie Jewels

Plop
in the middle of the path
a cow patty
bigger than a dinner plate

Smelly pie
sizzling
with blowfly raisins

Melting in the sun

How can you charm
these butterflies
dainty jewels
in sky-blue tights
to dance around
such disgusting pastry?

My net at the ready
I stand
pondering how
to swoop up the jewels

And leave the pie

Meeting on a Gravel Bar

It's just us, snake

Nobody here
to see what will happen
between us

You want by
I want your skin
You'll bite if you have to
I'll kill if I can

On this gravel bar
we'll test our skills
and none will know
of our courage

It's just us, snake

Let's do it

Looking Down Instead of Up

Oh no!
Good bull, nice bull.

N-i-i-i-ice bull.
I didn't see you here.
I didn't know
this was your field.

I won't wave my net anymore.
Okay?
I don't need that butterfly.
Okay?

I'm leaving now.
See?

Next time I'll go around.
Okay?

Good bull, n-i-i-i-ice bull.

Thank you!

Looking Up Instead of Down

Hawk?
Buzzard?
Hard to tell
that high.
There's another!
Pair of hawks?
Yes!
They're
landing
in those
trees!
I need
to get their
picture!
I need
to get out
of this field
before they
spot me!
I need
to run!
I need
to . . .
oh,
not
again!
I need to learn
to look down
instead of
up.

Today I Had To

Today I said it.

I said it when I wrecked my bike
on the gravel road
and crashed over the handlebars
and tore my Levi's
and cut both knees.

I rolled over
and kicked the bike away
hard as I could
and hugged my knees against the pain.

That's when I said it.

I hope I won't ever say it again
but today,
seemed like I had to.

Whose Tree Is This?

The tree of the owl
who dines on mouse
and drops fur bits
like table crumbs.

The tree of the owl
whose troll's mound
of broken bones
litters the moss.

The tree of the owl
should have a sign:

> If you're small
> be cautious
> beware
> look up!

Infield Chatter

Poem for Two Voices

Pitcher — *Shortstop*

Look at him
standing at the plate
swinging that bat
like a toothpick!

He's e-NORM-ous!

What's he doing
in a junior league?

He's got to be married
with kids *my age.*

Know why
they call this
the pitcher's mound?

It's a burial ground
for pitchers
killed by this guy.

Why is it so high?

To make you
a better target!
He's going to

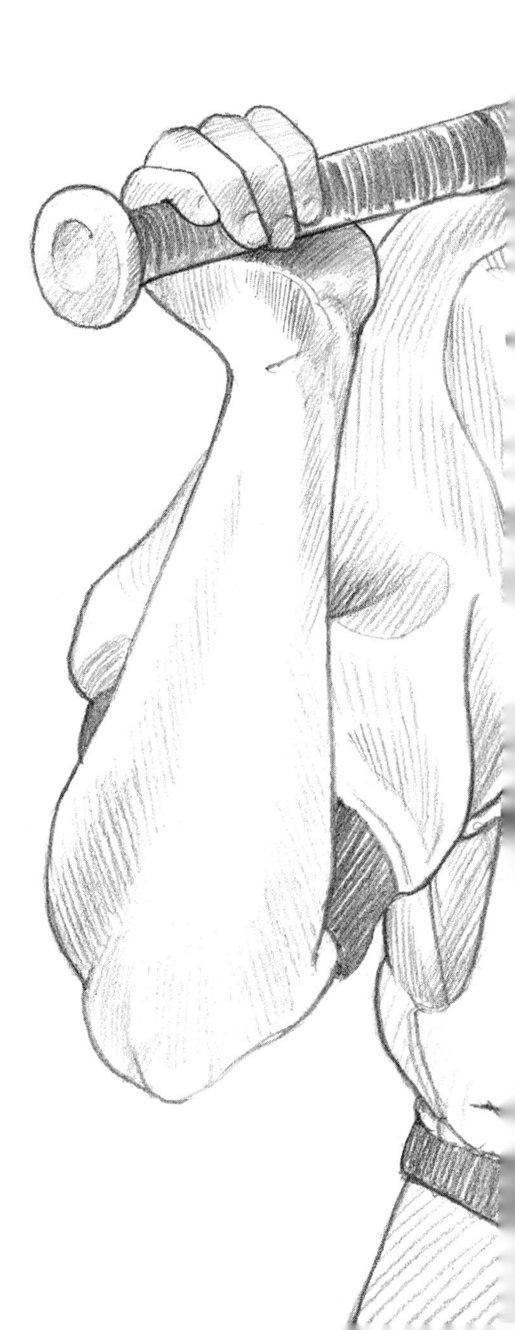

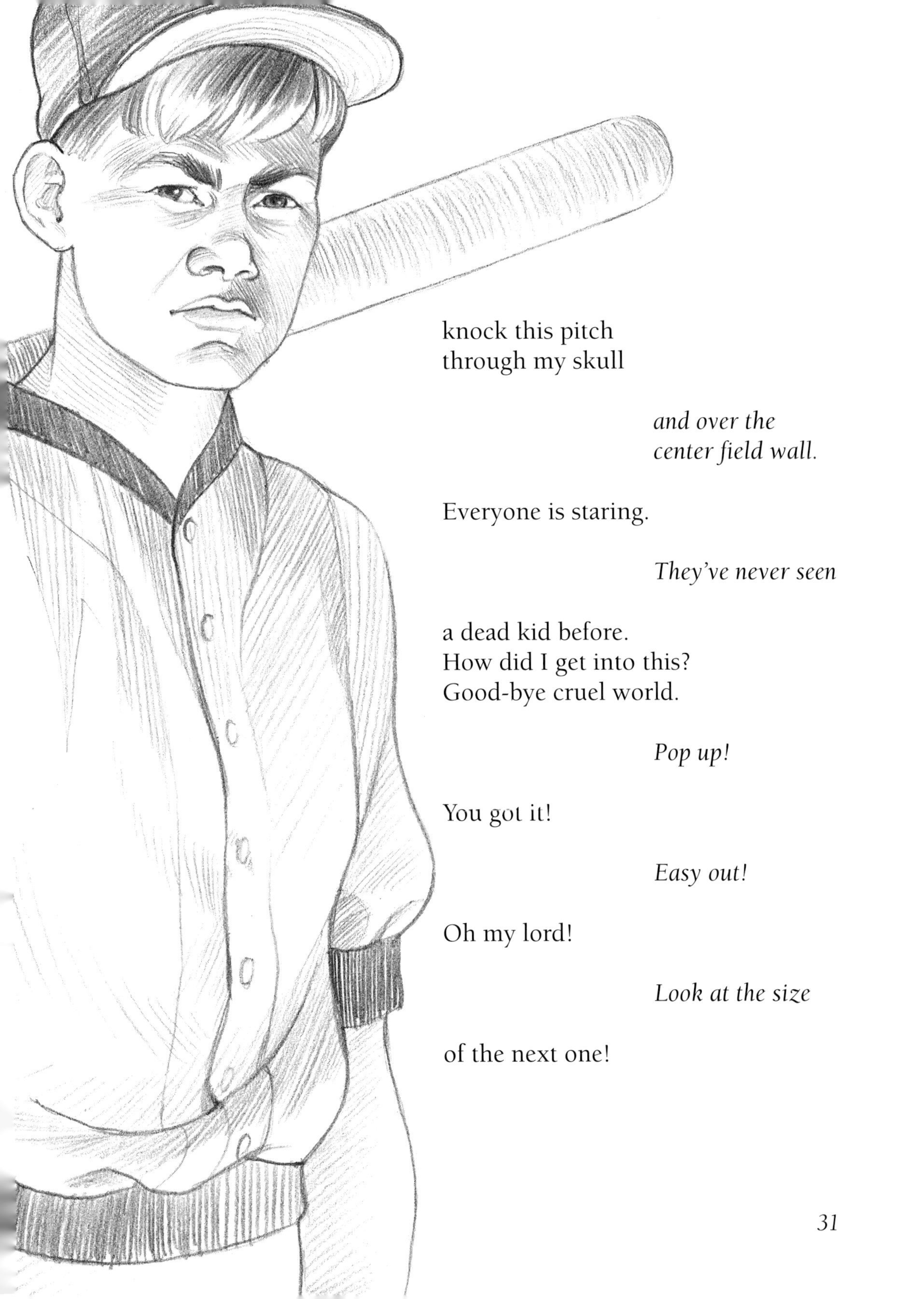

knock this pitch
through my skull

and over the
center field wall.

Everyone is staring.

They've never seen

a dead kid before.
How did I get into this?
Good-bye cruel world.

Pop up!

You got it!

Easy out!

Oh my lord!

Look at the size

of the next one!

Plate Talk

Poem for Two Voices

Batter *Catcher*

Oh man,
two outs, two on . . .

Fire it home, Johnny!
N-o-o-o hitter!

Down by one . . .
Why me?

High hard one!
Easy out!

He's seven-feet tall!
What do they feed him?

Batters like you.
Your insurance paid?

Huh!
Man, I didn't see it!

Like his slow one?
Try to stay loose.

Huh!
I think that sounded high!

He's getting wild.
Protect yourself!

Huh!
I hit it!
I hit it!

Pop up!

I hit it!

Shortstop!

I hit it!

He's out!

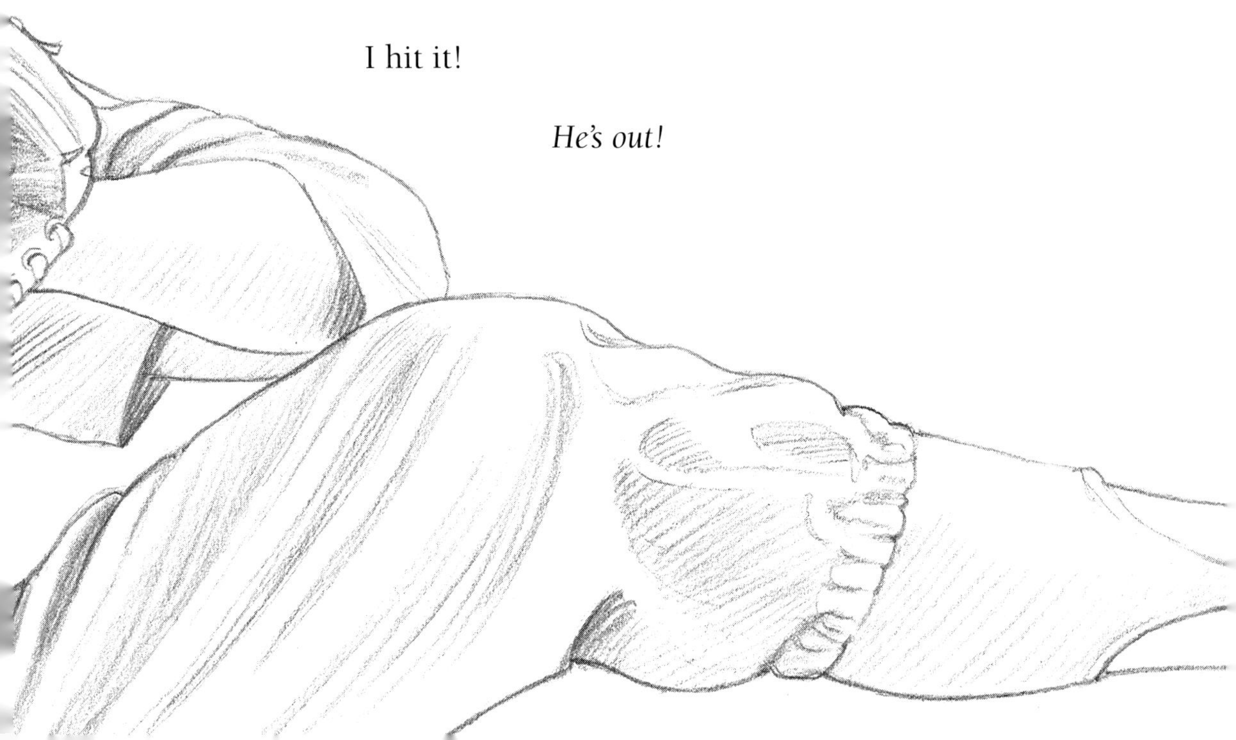

Market Bound

Mom's reading
Dad's driving
I'm in the back

We pass
a guy in a pickup
pulling a trailer
of cows

The trailer's filthy
The cows wide-eyed

We glide past

They press together
nostrils flared
against the wind

market bound.

Footprints

Once
the beast paused here
where I stand,
raised its great head,
sniffed for danger
or food,
moved on,

Leaving in the clay
a single footprint
to prove it was here.

I stand where it stood,
look where it looked,
and wonder
what I can do
to leave a footprint
to prove I was here.

Qualities of Darkness

I snap off my light
and think,
a cave has its own kind
of darkness.

It swallows me
down its black throat,
blinds me
in a sightless universe.
Dripping notes
in invisible pools
sound far-off, enchanted.

My room at night
is dark, too,
but different, reassuring.
I can feel-see my way,
and plinking sink notes
are familiar.

Darkness on a river?
Frogs,
mosquitoes
under a bowl of stars.

Darkness is shivery,
scary,
when it's shut
behind eyelids

squeezed
against fear

But it's also cracks
of excitement
through laced fingers
in hide-and-go-seek.

Slick with mud
from the comfortless
stone floor,
I press on the switch
and turn, following
the strong line of light
holding back
the darkness.

Journal Entry

Found this perfect pond
deep in the woods.

Amazing!

Caught a dragonfly.

Scared three bullfrogs
into the water.

Something ran off
through the trees.

Kneeling beside deer tracks
in the soft mud,
I felt at home.

A Chip of Flint

See this?
Too thin
for an arrowhead.

Maybe a chip
from the weapon
being made
by a master craftsman,
flint in one hand
antler tip in the other,
strong wrists
fashioning
a new stone point.

Did he pause
in these woods
silent, alone
or was he surrounded
by chuckling comrades
who winked at secrets
as flint chips fell?

It doesn't matter
the chip was rejected
by the arrowhead.

I accept it
as a gift
from an unknown hand.

Confidence

The mosquito is
sneaky
a smug vampire
who
bites first
then sings in your ear

The honeybee
can hurt you but
obviously
prefers not to
and buzzes
fairly
so you'll know
he's about

The wasp?
Sinister
armed and dangerous
on the most-wanted list
The scorpion
if he could fly
would be a wasp

The bumblebee
is the most confident
He knows he's got
what it takes
and he knows
you know

That's what
confidence
is all about

Beginner's Luck

With the sun in my eyes
I saw . . .
What?
Something there
high in the tree.
Black?
Starling?
I couldn't see.

Holding my Christmas gun
in my hands,
I wanted a test.
If I pumped enough,
could I hit a pest
that far from me?

The trigger tightened,
snapped,
the pellet flew.

Pleased,
I watched the bird
bounce,
fall from the tree

And ran to find
my trophy,
cardinal,
songbird,
dead!

I buried it
vowing I'd never again
aim
when I could not see.

Home-grown

Tenderly,
fingers lingering
over wondrous gifts,
peeling
    paring
        slicing,
he contemplates with satisfaction
the completed act.

"Nothing beats home-grown,"
he says.
"You won't find corn this sweet
in any store."

Another platter,
meaty red slabs
surprisingly heavy
on white china.
"Try these tomatoes,
tell me these aren't
the best you ever tasted."

Sweet onions served
with garden talk,
language of the soil,
wisdom of grandfathers.

Golden ears
dripping butter,

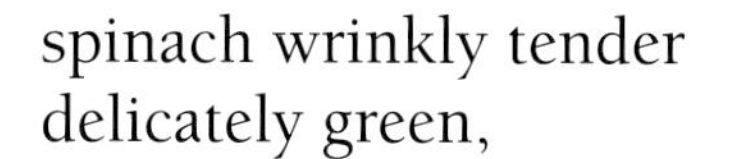

spinach wrinkly tender
delicately green,

Cauliflower better than
expected,
green beans
demanding
to be bragged on.

"You won't find these
in any store,"
he says
to heads bobbing
over full plates.

He nods,
agreeing with himself.
I smile and think,
"Nothing beats home-grown."

A Question of Control

If you need
to be
in control

Don't ride a
horse

A horse does not
understand
that

Concept

The Fisherman

Fishing off a riverbank
is the only way to go

Sitting on soft grass
legs dangling
five feet above the water

Half a sack of cookies and
two apples left

Been snagged for an hour

No chance of being bothered
by a fish

Fishing off a riverbank
is the only way to go

Bright-Eyed Good-byes

Birds
busily
tidying up
the season

Shouting
bright-eyed
good-byes

Joining
choosing sides
forming teams

Arguing
about plans

Debating
from treetops

Everyone
talking
at once

Swirling
down
to the lawns
like black leaves
for last
snacks

Gusting
skyward

Diving
wheeling
practicing

Days
of false
starts

Where
is the leader?

Who
is in charge?

When
was the signal?

I
missed the vote
same as always

They're gone!

The Purchase of Small Secrets

Along this bank
I'll make no sound
this afternoon

My reward will be

Snake swimming
unconcerned
across the river

Crow
cautious
tracking mud
dining on turtle

Carp rolling
lazy
ripples

Muskrat paddling
unaware
unafraid

My reward will be

The purchase
of small secrets

Well worth the price
of an afternoon
of silence